Marcus P Norton

In Memoriam

Memorial services in honor of James Abram Garfield. Second Edition

Marcus P Norton

In Memoriam
Memorial services in honor of James Abram Garfield. Second Edition

ISBN/EAN: 9783337092900

Printed in Europe, USA, Canada, Australia, Japan

Cover: Foto ©Raphael Reischuk / pixelio.de

More available books at **www.hansebooks.com**

Very Truly Yours
J. A. Garfield.

In Memoriam.

MEMORIAL SERVICES

IN HONOR OF

JAMES ABRAM GARFIELD,

The Twentieth President of the United States.

HELD AT SEA,

ON THE CUNARD STEAMSHIP "SCYTHIA,"

SEPTEMBER 26, 1881.

Hon. MARCUS P. NORTON,
OF NEW YORK AND BOSTON,
CHAIRMAN.

LEWIS C. LILLIE,
OF NEW YORK AND BOSTON,
SECRETARY.

Second Edition.

BOSTON:
FRANKLIN PRESS: RAND, AVERY, & CO.
1882.

AUTHOR'S NOTE.

Of the first edition of the book, — giving an account of the " MEMORIAL SERVICES " held at sea on the twenty-sixth day of September, 1881, in honor of JAMES ABRAM GARFIELD, the assassinated President, — there were twelve hundred copies printed. One thousand copies of that edition were forwarded to those persons who subscribed for the same while passengers on board the CUNARD *Steamship* " SCYTHIA," in the main saloon of which those impressive and interesting services were held.

I have thought it best to issue another edition in order to supply the demand. There have been a very few verbal changes made in some of the Addresses, especially so in that by the CHAIRMAN, which was written in a hurried manner, just before the assembling of the passengers in the MAIN SA-LOON at 2 o'clock afternoon of the same day.

During that writing the winds were very strong, and the great ship was rocking about on the waves of an angry sea — hence I have felt justified in making corrections in that address, and in giving to others an opportunity to make such corrections in their addresses, respectively, as they might desire.

Both editions have been issued without any compensation in money or of property value, or the hope of any, from any source whatever. If this little volume shall be of use or benefit to any one, and carry with it honorable remembrances and kindly feelings through the coming years, and serve in some degree to perpetuate in the hearts of the living the honored name, as well as the honorable life, of the great and illustrious dead, whose earthly life was closed at ELBERON, in New Jersey, in the month of September, A.D. 1881, by a fatal wound received at the hands of an assassin in the capital of the American Union on the second day of July, 1881, at a railway station, I shall be glad, and more than compensated for all the time, care, and expense of it.

MARCUS P. NORTON.

BOSTON, MASS., June 14, 1882.

CONTENTS.

Memorial Services.

In compliance with the following proclamation and notice, more than two hundred and fifty passengers, representing Europe and America, assembled at two o'clock in the afternoon of Sept. 26, 1881, in the main SALOON of the steamship " Scythia," which was appropriately draped and arranged for the solemn occasion : —

By the President of the United States of America:

A PROCLAMATION.

Whereas, In his inscrutable wisdom, it has pleased God to remove from us the illustrious head of the nation, JAMES A. GARFIELD, late President of the United States ; and

Whereas, It is fitting that the deep grief which fills all hearts should manifest itself with one accord toward the throne of Infinite Grace, and that we should bow before the Almighty and seek from him that consolation in our affliction and that sanctification of our loss which he is able and willing to vouchsafe ;

Now, therefore, in obedience to sacred duty, and in accordance with the desire of the people, I, CHESTER A. ARTHUR, President of the United States of America, do hereby appoint Monday next, the twenty-sixth day of September, on which day the remains of our honored and beloved dead will be consigned to their last resting-place on earth, to be observed throughout the United States as a day of humiliation and mourning; and I earnestly recommend all the people to assemble on that day in their respective places of divine worship, there to render alike their tribute of sorrowful submission to the will of Almighty God, and of reverence and love for the memory and character of our late chief magistrate.

In witness whereof I have hereunto set my hand, and caused the seal of the United States to be affixed.

Done at the city of Washington, the twenty-second day of September, in the year of our Lord 1881, and of the independence of the United States the one hundred and sixth.

CHESTER A. ARTHUR.

By the President:

[SEAL.] JAMES G. BLAINE, *Secretary of State.*

NOTICE.

" *Capt.* MURPHY, in command of the steamship ' SCYTHIA,' having kindly and generously consented, notice is hereby given to all persons on board this steamship, that, in compliance with the proclamation of his Excellency CHESTER A. ARTHUR, President of the United States of America, dated the twenty-second day of September, A.D. 1881, and also in conformity to the known wishes of a very large number of passengers now on shipboard, MEMORIAL SERVICES will be held at two o'clock in the afternoon of to-day in the main saloon of the ' SCYTHIA,' in honor and to the memory of JAMES A. GARFIELD, late President of said United States, who, after a long, painful, and heroic struggle for health and for life, died in the seventh month of the first year of his presidential term of a fatal wound received at the hands of an assassin in the capital of his country on the morning of the second day of July, A.D. 1881.

" All persons are invited to be present on the occasion hereinbefore stated, and to take part in such proceedings as shall then and there be deemed proper while a great nation is in mourning."

At the appointed hour, and amid the deepest silence, the *Rev.* JOHN P. NEWMAN, D.D., LL.D., of *New York*, said, —

As this day has been designated by *President* ARTHUR to be observed with fitting religious and civic services expressive of our great loss in the sad death of *Gen.* JAMES A. GARFIELD, it is eminently proper that we should gather here in mid-ocean, and unite with our countrymen at home and in all lands in paying a tribute of respect to the memory of the illustrious dead, and in offering our prayers to Almighty God for the bereaved family, and for our stricken but still beloved country. I have therefore, on the part of your committee, the pleasure and the honor to announce as chairman for this memorable occasion the Hon. MARCUS P. NORTON, of New York, who will now take the chair.

The impressive services were commenced with the well-known hymn, —

"NEARER, MY GOD, TO THEE."

. "Nearer, my God, to thee,
　　Nearer to thee!
　E'en though it be a cross
　　That raiseth me;
　Still, all my song shall be, —
　Nearer, my God, to thee,
　　Nearer to thee!

"Though, like the wanderer,
　　The sun gone down,
　Darkness be over me,
　　My rest a stone;
　Yet in my dreams I'd be
　Nearer, my God, to thee,
　　Nearer to thee!

"There let the way appear
　　Steps unto heaven;
　All that thou sendest me
　　In mercy given;
　Angels to beckon me
　Nearer, my God, to thee,
　　Nearer to thee!

"Then with my waking thoughts,
　　Bright with thy praise,
　Out of my stony griefs
　　Bethel I'll raise;
　So by my woes to be
　Nearer, my God, to thee,
　　Nearer to thee!"

Mrs. Bolton conducted the singing of this hymn, and played the Harmonium in a very effective and solemn manner.

An impressive and touching prayer was then offered by the Rev. James M. King, D.D., of New York.

Then came the addresses of the following-named gentlemen in the succession or order stated : *to wit,* —

1. *Judge* Marcus P. Norton, of New York, N.Y.
2. *Judge* Charles A. Peabody, of New York, N.Y.
3. *Bishop* H. N. McTyeire, of Nashville, Tenn.
4. *Judge* John L. Rose, Little Rock, Ark.
5. *Judge* E. H. East, of Nashville, Tenn.
6. *Rev. Father* M. I. Masterson, of Peabody, Mass.
7. *Hon.* Agustus Belmont, of New York, N.Y.
8. Resolutions offered by *Gen.* Cyrus Bussey, President of Board of Chamber of Commerce of New Orleans, La.
9. Resolutions offered by *Gen.* Bussey, seconded by *Hon.* F. A. Ward, of Brooklyn, N.Y.
10. *Gen.* Cyrus Bussey's Address in support of the resolutions offered by him.
11. Address by *Hon.* F. A. Ward, of Brooklyn, N.Y., upon seconding the resolutions offered by *Gen.* Bussey.
12. Singing of the hymn, "My country, 'tis of thee," etc.
13. A motion by *Rev. Dr.* John P. Newman for adjournment.
14. Announcement by the Chairman that the resolution for adjournment had been agreed to.
15. Adjournment *sine die.*

A RECORD IN BRIEF OF GENERAL JAMES A. GARFIELD, — A CONVENIENT SUMMARY.

At 14 he was at work at a carpenter's bench.

At 16 he was a boatman on the Ohio canal.

At 18 he was studying in the Chester (Ohio) Seminary.

At 21 he was teaching in one of Ohio's common schools, pushing forward with his own studies at the same time.

At 23 he entered Williams College.

At 26 he graduated from Williams with the highest honors of his class.

At 27 he was tutor at Hiram College, Ohio.

At 28 he was principal of Hiram College.

At 29 he was a member of the Ohio Senate, — the youngest member of that body.

At 30 he was Colonel of the 42d Ohio Regiment.

At 31 he was placed in command of a brigade, routed the Confederates under Humphrey Marshall, helped Gen. Buell in his fight at Pittsburg Landing, played a prominent part in the siege of Corinth and in the important movements along the Memphis and Charleston Railroad.

At 32 he was appointed chief of staff of the Army of the Cumberland, participated in the campaign in Middle Tennessee and in the notable battle of Chickamauga, and was promoted to the rank of Major-General for gallant conduct and valuable services upon the battle-field.

At 33 he was in Congress, the successor of Joshua R. Giddings deceased.

At 48, having been continued in Congress since he was 33, a period of about eighteen years, he was elected to the United States Senate.

At 49 he was nominated for the Presidency of the United

States by the National Convention of the Republican party, held at the city of Chicago, in the State of Illinois, in the summer of 1880.

At 50 he was elected President, and inaugurated at the city of Washington at 12 o'clock noon of the fourth day of March, 1881; and July 2, 1881, was shot by GUITEAU, in the "Baltimore and Potomac Railroad Depot," in the city of Washington, — the CAPITAL, — who inflicted a dangerous wound, which, after great suffering, proved to be a fatal one.

Sept. 19, 1881, President GARFIELD died at ELBERON, *Long Branch*, State of New Jersey, of the fatal wound received from the *assassin* GUITEAU's pistol.

Sept. 20, 1881, the *deceased* PRESIDENT was removed from *Elberon* to the ROTUNDA in the CAPITOL at Washington.

Sept. 23, 1881, his remains were removed from Washington to the city of *Cleveland*, OHIO, preparatory for burial services.

Sept. 26, 1881, BURIAL SERVICES were held at Cleveland, Ohio, near MENTOR, his rural home; and on the same day the dead President was committed to a VAULT in LAKE VIEW Cemetery, near by the city of Cleveland.

ADDRESS

OF

HON. MARCUS P. NORTON.

OFFICE ADDRESS:

Nos. 6 AND 7 BOWDOIN SQUARE,

BOSTON, MASS.

CHAIRMAN UPON THE OCCASION OF "MEMORIAL SERVICES,"
HELD AT SEA, ON THE CUNARD STEAMSHIP
"SCYTHIA," SEPTEMBER 26, 1881,

IN HONOR OF

JAMES ABRAM GARFIELD,

The Twentieth President of the United States.

ADDRESS.

Ladies and Gentlemen, — Called as I have been by your politeness and kindness to preside over your deliberations on this sad occasion, I have to thank you, and shall hope at least to meet your wishes in conducting your proceedings, and in executing the duties you have assigned to me at this time upon this beautiful steamship making her voyage so well and successfully over the great and troubled deep from England to America.

The eyes of the great Republic and those of every civilized nation upon the earth are to-day turned towards the city of Cleveland, in Ohio, where the solemn and impressive services of the Church are being pronounced over all that remains on the earth of *Gen.* James A. Garfield, the twentieth President of the United States.

Born in the humble walks of life — by a praiseworthy ambition, backed by an energetic industry; by sound common-sense, and by honesty and uprightness in his life and in his manner of living — he obtained

17

a thorough education; became master of the sciences and of the languages; well read in the history of the world, and, forcing his way onward in life's great highway, he surmounted all obstacles before him (and they were many), and came to the head and full command of one of the divisions of the armies of the Republic he loved so well, bearing the emblems and having the authority of a major-general in the service of the United States, by virtue of a commission issued by the War Department and signed by the immortal Lincoln. Still onward and onward he made his course in life's toilsome way; and while he held the great commission of a major-general, his constituency elected him to the Congress of the United States by large and overwhelming majorities; and while the nation and the union of States were still in imminent danger, in the midst of a great, aye, the most gigantic, civil war ever upon the earth, — a war largely demanding the sacrifice of life and of property, and requiring unexampled expenditures of the people's money to save that Union, the Republic, and the Constitution from the hands of disunion and rebellion, — he entered the House of Representatives of the American Congress, and there, through a succession of elections by the people of his native State, for eighteen years faithfully and fearlessly defended the right; aye, in those years he gallantly and patriotically defended his imperilled country, her flag, and her Constitution, both in war and in peace, and did much to preserve the integrity and to maintain the prosperity, and to advance the glory of the arms of the United States of America as one undivided and inseparable union of States.

While in Congress he was ever and firmly on the side of the largest liberty. He was true to his country, to its flag, and to its government. So, also, he was faithful and true to the people, whether rich or poor, and he always gave a helping hand to those struggling to obtain their rights. So much was he loved and admired by those with whom he associated in Congress, that he soon became a distinguished leader in his party there, which he maintained inviolate through those long years of anxious and troublesome times, until from the House of Representatives he went to the UNITED STATES SENATE, by a very decided majority-vote of the Legislature of OHIO, his native State.

While he was Ohio's chosen SENATOR in the nation's great Legislature, he was nominated by his party at Chicago, in 1880, for the Presidential office, and being in November of that year triumphantly elected by the people, he was subsequently sworn into that high office; and thereupon, at twelve o'clock, noon, on the fourth day of March, 1881, at the Capital of a great and prosperous nation, he became the *twentieth* President of the United States of America, amid the ringing of bells, the firing of cannon, and the exulting joy and universal thanksgivings of the American people.

He commenced his administration in the midst of very bright, favorable, and most beautiful auspices. Peace prevailed in each and all of the States. The Union had been permanently re-established. The Great Republic was resting on solid rock. The American charter of human liberty — the Constitution — had been enlarged and sustained. The people in every part of our country were pursuing peaceful ways. Lasting prosperity was spread out before them on every hand. Men of all political parties, of all church creeds, of professional life, of mechanical, of commercial, and of agricultural pursuits, seemed to vie with each other, and to be well pleased with home, and satisfied with their country and its government. The great nation stood forth in all her beauty, in her grandeur, and in her mighty power. From every mountain top, from every hillside, and from every valley there went up to heaven — to God — one grand and universal song of joy and gladness, in that a new era of peace, of purity, and of prosperity, in and for *the whole* country, North and South, East and West, had been thus so well inaugurated, and the people everywhere in all the States of the American Republic rejoiced, and happily exclaimed — AMEN !

He had not gone far in the presidential office to which he had thus been elected and inaugurated and commissioned to fill for four years by the people, when lo! on one beautiful morning, — the closing day of the week, — when on his way in a peaceful, lawful, and rightful manner to pay a visit of love and loyal devotion to his excellent and noble wife, — who but a few short days before had arisen from a long and dangerous illness at the executive mansion, and had gone to obtain renewed health and strength from the sea-air at Long Branch, — he, the lawful and exalted President of a great, a peaceful, and yet powerful nation, was shot down in blood and fatal wound by a cowardly assassin, at a railway-station in the capital of his country, and near unto the very shadow of the executive mansion he had but a few moments before left so full of hope, of happiness, and glowing health.

For nearly three months of intense pain and agony of suffering, — and with the aid of the very best of physicians and surgeons that could be produced in the United States, — he manfully, patiently, and most bravely struggled against a fatal wound for recovery

and for life. But it was not in the power of those
learned and eminent physicians, aided as they were
at all times by the devotion, the immediate pres-
ence, and the constant care of his brave and ever-
faithful wife, — his true — his *heroic* wife. For at
last, when believing him to be somewhat improving,
and all had gone to a night's repose — doctors, wife,
and all — save his trusted and faithful friend-attend-
ants, there, in the silent watches of *that* night, he
suddenly awoke from that which had been pronounced by attendants and doctors to be a quiet
sleep, and reaching forth his weak and trembling
hand, made his last audible prayer upon the earth,
and it was, " Oh, this is terrible pain! *Swaim*, can
you not do something for me? Oh, SWAIM!" With
this, his agonizing prayer, just spoken by him, he
came to the margin of the narrow river, and, cross
ing over, completed the journey of life. In the still
and solemn hours of the night he parted from wife
and their loved children ; from his aged mother,
whom he saluted with an affectionate kiss at his
inauguration ; from everybody, aye, from earth itself, he took an untimely departing ; and paying a
long farewell to all — and to life upon the earth —
vacated the presidential chair. Yes, in those silent
hours of that ever-to-be-remembered night he quietly
drew about himself the drapery of his couch, and,

without uttering another word after his fervent prayer
for help, passed out and into the dark valley, — into
the shadow of death ; and very soon thereafter that
eminent physician and surgeon, Dr. BLISS, announced
to those there, and to all the world, " It is over. He
is dead!" Garfield dead? Yes; and oh, how great
the havoc that death hath wrought!

To-day our great nation is in tears at the grave of
its illustrious dead. She is heavily dressed in mourning: for in every State, in every city, village, and
hamlet of that prosperous country, her beautiful and
honored flag is flying at half-mast; while upon all
her public buildings, and upon all the public buildings of the thirty-seven States and eleven Territories
of the Union, as well as upon thousands and thousands of homes in all parts of the land, among the
rich and among the poor, may at this hour be seen
the emblems of sorrow, — real, deep sorrow. And
there, too, may be seen the tears of universal grief
because their great chief and leader has fallen in
death by the assassin, and at this time is being conveyed to the narrow subterraneous cavern of earth, to
dwell among the dead until that day when, with one ·
foot upon the sea and the other upon the land, the
angel of the Lord our God shall proclaim time to be
no more.

How grand, how beautiful, and how brave he was

on the shores of the great ocean at Long Branch in the midst of the most intense suffering and physical weakness, when, day after day, his stout and manly · form wasted away like as the summer's sun and heat take away the waters of forest lands, of rivers, and of the sea. There he looked out upon the blue waves of the mighty deep, with his loving wife still side by side with him, while she silently watched the ebbing and flowing of the tide of human life. Thus situated, he takes her by the hand, and exclaims, " This — *this* is glorious, CRETE ! " and then and there this great man made another effort for the mastery over death and the grave. In that struggle he forgot neither the beautiful in nature nor the love of a devoted wife, or of noble children, or of an aged and loving mother ; or of home, or of his country and the American people, whose great and honored President he was. *That* outlooking of his upon the face of the ocean whose waters separate vast empires, kingdoms, and republics from our great American Union of Republican States, and the life-effort of his, and those words of good cheer, were almost the last with him ; for he was far nearer the dividing line that separates earth's flying years from that beautiful land along whose shores falls that heavenly light which cometh from the sun of an everlasting righteousness.

From a scene like this we stand back in wonderful

amazement. We look again, and this illustrious son of America has gone, — gone to his eternal rest, to an everlasting peace, and to an heavenly reward; and, after life's fitful dream, he sleeps, and sleeps well. The battle of life has been fought, and a brilliant and abiding victory won by him. In a calm and quiet peace let him rest.

> " Death makes no conquest of the conqueror,
>   For now he lives in fame, though not in life."

To-day his eyes, glazed and dimmed by the hand of death, see not the gathering throng of his countrymen, as in solemn procession they come near the family home to aid in the sad business of placing him in final rest and in the quiet and undisturbed peace of the grave. His ears, heavily laden in the stillness of the hour, hear not the foot-falls in the sanctuary to-day — in that far away beautiful city in our native land — of loving ones, of devoted friends, or of his loyal, weeping countrymen. Oh, no! for it is a sad hour to mother, to wife, to children, and to friends; for the last great enemy of man hath come and made desolate a beautiful and a happy home, extinguished forever a great and brilliant light, and put a great nation into mourning.

The flowers of spring-time and of summer hours are passing away, and the frosts of winter are now approaching. These, all these, and all things else of earth, shall come and go through the coming centuries ; but, my countrymen, and citizens of other nations, now and here assembled, I beg to remind you that beyond all doubt the name of GARFIELD will ever live and be honored at home and in other lands. It is imperishable, because it is immortal.

Peacefully shall rest this great man, lifted as he was from an humble station in life to the very highest and most exalted in the gift of a great and generous people ; and from the North, from the South, from the East, and from the West, through all time, shall come those of our countrymen to place flowers around and upon his grave ; and there — in grateful recollection of his grand and beautiful home-life, of his manly virtues, of his loyal devotion to his country, of his generous care for the poor and those struggling for their natural and their lawful rights, and for his every good quality of head and heart — pay tribute to his memory, while unbidden and almost unconsciously shall fall burning tears of attachment, of admiration, and of love. Aye, the Union, the country, and its government he so much loved and so well served ; which he so greatly honored, and in whose best interests he gave up his life, shall, at a time not far away, erect a monument to his memory more lasting and enduring than brass, to mark the place where sleeps in death the second martyred President of the United States of America.

His features shall be chiselled in marble, they shall be cast in bronze, and delineated upon the canvas. In the public parks and gardens of the nation; in her chosen halls and in her libraries, the marble, the bronze, and the well-made painting, — showing the face and the form of this great scholar, general, representative, senator, president, and statesman, and, above all, an honest man; aye, higher still, a Christian gentleman, — shall be placed by a loving and generous people; so that, all those who shall come in the long succession of generations yet to be may see thus represented he whom the historian then shall have assigned one of the best and brightest pages in history, close by those occupied by WASHINGTON, by the illustrious LINCOLN, by GRANT, — the greatest general of any time or country, — and also close to those of other great and noble men who, in their time, largely contributed to make the grand and beautiful history of the American Republic, and to perpetuate the union of the States, inseparable, indivisible, — one grand, glorious, and united whole for all the centuries yet to come.

AMERICANS! our country is this day in tears; she is sadly burdened with a great sorrow, and deeply stricken with an unwelcome grief. In that great country — extending from ocean to ocean, over a distance of about three thousand six hundred miles from east to west, and of more than two thousand miles from the Canadian Dominion, on the north, and the Gulf of Mexico and the Mexican Republic, on the south — thousands and thousands of bells are symbolizing the sorrow and the grief of the people; and mourning representations are everywhere to be seen, because of this great, this sad, event, whereby the President sees, hears, and speaks never again.

But GARFIELD, though dead, yet he lives, and will ever live in the hearts and memory of the people, — of all the people of the great Republic, now firmly and forever re-united and sent onward in her great mission, to be the light, the admiration, and the guiding-star of the nations, kingdoms, and empires of the world. Heaven bless to-day, and ever, our sorrowing, weeping country.

AMERICANS! how grand, how beautiful and heart-reaching, has the Queen of England conducted herself, in her personal capacity as well as that of the sovereign ruler of a great and truly noble people, towards the wife, the children, and family of our now death-stricken chief, and also towards our country in its entirety, and the people of the United States of America. So, too, has England — industrious in mechanical, agricultural, commercial, and other pursuits; wealthy and powerful and royal — been very kind and full of sympathy towards the great Republic and the grief-stricken family of the dead President. By these acts — gracious and kind as they are — England has bound herself a thousand times more closely to the American people; and her exalted and high-minded Queen — already very highly esteemed by our countrymen in every part of the Union — has brought herself and her people more closely to our hearts, and to our nation's admiration and love. Thus has she honored herself, her royal family, her government, and all her people, and forever made for herself and for them a place in the American heart and among the American people. Let us never forget this noble Queen, this wise, this dignified and beloved ruler, nor that land and great people she governs and loves so well.

But though our great President has fallen by the assassin's blow, and passed forever beyond our sight into the silent chambers of the grave, his name shall be embalmed in American hearts; it shall stand in full view in characters of living light in the gratitude of a wonderful people and nation; and it shall ever have an abiding-place in the history of these days and times, and in the history of the world, as well as in marble, in bronze, and on the canvas, along with those of our Washington, of Lincoln, of Grant, and other Americans who — by acts of wisdom, of love, of truth, and of patriotism — have challenged the admiration of the world in making their country great and grand before all nations and rulers, and in securing the liberty, the prosperity, the happiness, and the peace of their countrymen for the present and for all the years that the future shall bring.

General GARFIELD was great in life; he was patient and uncomplaining in the midst of the most intense suffering in mind and in body; but still more great, patient, and grand in death. From the earth he came, and to the earth he this day is returned; while the ever living life which he had, is this hour, we hope and trust, safely housed in that house having many mansions, not made with hands, but eternal in the heavens, whose maker and builder is Christ our Saviour, — " our elder Brother."

Though his death fills the heart of our nation with sorrow and deep grief; yet it and the people he loved and served so well, will no doubt, advance in grandeur and in greatness through his seemingly untimely death. How or wherein is not for me on this occasion to discuss. Hereafter it will appear to you. Of the politics of our country I will not this day speak to you. It were not just or proper that I should; but at the open grave of the illustrious Garfield, with you this day I stand as a mourner, and my tears flow and mingle with yours, and with those of our countrymen.

To establish his claim to superior abilities needs no eulogium from us ; to render his name immortal, no monument that man can rear. The works of his public and of his private life praise him, and will perpetuate his fame and his memory while the present is ever passing and future years come and go.

Again the great lesson is repeated, and we are at this hour impressed that superior talents, extensive usefulness, great honors, or rank, or exalted station cannot stay the approach of death — for we do know that GARFIELD hath fallen in the battle of life at the head of the Great Republic, the leader and ruler of a nation and people, respected, loved, and honored by all civilized nations and peoples in the Old World as well as in the New, and that this day all of him underneath the arch-dome of the heavens above us that is earthy will be committed to the earth, and there to have —

> " The icy worm around him steal,
> Without the power to scare away
> The cold consumer of his clay."

His sad, very sad, death has a lesson for all. His virtues and talents; his energy and perseverance ; his love of home and of country, and his every manly quality of head and heart are this day recommended to be imitated by us, — by Americans and Europeans everywhere, as well as by everybody the world over, by the radiance reflected from his tomb.

That he had no faults is not pretended; for had he been without these in such a life as is this mortal, earthly life of ours, then he would not have been man. His failings will, they must, be forgotten, and his virtues and good examples be indelibly written on the tablet of memory.

" *De mortuis nil nisi bonum,*"
as well as
" *De mortuis nil nisi verum.*"

Brief, indeed, is the time since GENERAL GARFIELD stood before his loyal countrymen, holding, in official place, their highest trust, and enjoying their unlimited confidence, honored and admired by them. But how is it this day? Then he was like

" Some tall cliff, that lifts its awful form,
   Swells from the vale, and midway leaves the storm,
   Though around its breast the rolling clouds are spread,
   Eternal sunshine settles on its head."

But to-day the civilized nations of the earth, and the people of all climes, as well as we who are here assembled, are admonished that, after all, earth is not our home; that " earth's stormy nights will soon be over " with all now living, and that it is not " all of life to live, or of death to die." The great destroyer comes in God's own appointed time and manner, and leaves no palace, no home, and no place untouched. The rich and the poor, the educated and the uneducated, those in freedom's air and those enslaved; those in prison and those out of prison, and those of exalted rank as well as those of lower degree, — all, all wither and perish when the cold night of death cometh. And so it was with the great President now deceased, whose name and memory we have come hither this day to respect and to honor in the manner so beautifully and touchingly suggested and recommended by the Proclamation of *President* AR-THUR, as best we may, although in mid-ocean we are homeward bound upon the waters of the mighty deep; for the dark night of death came about him with its chilling frosts, and they touched him, and he faded, withered, and fell, as fade, wither, and fall autumn leaves; but, though he has thus gone from earth away, his name and his memory perish not, for

> " Earth's transitory things decay ;
> Its pomps, its pleasures pass away ;
> But the sweet memory of the good
> Survives in the vicissitude.

> " As, in the heavens, the urns divine
> Of golden light forever shine ;
> Though clouds may darken, storms may rage,
> They still shine on from age to age ;

> " So, through the ocean-tide of years,
> The memory of the just appears ;
> So, through the tempest and the gloom,
> The good man's virtues light the tomb."

The mantle that he cast off at the gates of death has by our Constitution and laws fallen upon another. And to-day — while the illustrious dead chief is being borne away to the silent home of the dead, and buried from the sight of his loved ones ; from friends and from his countrymen — America has a rightful and lawful President, quietly and peacefully performing the functions of that high, dignified, and truly responsible office.

That mantle could not have fallen upon *a nobler* and *truer* man than *General* CHESTER A. ARTHUR. He is a good lawyer, holding high position, and of superior rank or order in his profession. He is a citizen of unclouded reputation, bearing before him an honest life and goodly living. He is well learned in his profession, is finely educated, and is an accomplished gentleman. He is well informed in the politics of our country, and familiar with official life and its burdensome duties. All in all, he is a firm, reliable, and upright citizen of our Republic now in tears at the grave of *General* JAMES A. GARFIELD, who died at the post of duty, the twentieth President of the United States of America.

Once before — and not many years ago — our country was called to a similar sorrow, when the illustrious LINCOLN, chief magistrate of the Republic, gave up his life by an assassin while taking rest from the cares and excitement of those perilous, stormy, and most unhappy times at a public and a respectable place of amusement at the capital of the nation. The Republic was then passing through the fire, and smoke, and blood of the greatest of all wars known in the history of the world. Then there was unrest in every part of our country. The fire and smoke of fierce battle were seen here and there. The rattle of musketry and clash of arms were heard in all directions. Not so when *President* GARFIELD fell at the hands of *another* assassin; for the great civil strife had passed into history, and peace prevailed in every part of the country.

General ARTHUR has succeeded to the office of PRESIDENT in a constitutional manner; and he is therefore the *twenty-first* PRESIDENT of the United States. He will in all things faithfully and honestly administer the affairs of the government and of our country. He will labor to perpetuate the union of the States, to make our country prosperous, and to lead the people of the whole country in peaceful ways and honorable pursuits. His address at the taking of the oath prescribed by our Constitution, though brief, is full of sound common-sense, and of wisdom, and of patriotism. Those words came from an honest heart. They cannot fail to satisfy everybody as to his qualifications and fitness to fill this great office, and to hold sacred all important trusts now devolved upon him by the operation of the laws of our country. In his administration the country will advance in business, commercial, and domestic affairs, as well as in foreign relations; and her resources will continue to be successfully developed for the good of the nation and of the people.

Ladies and Gentlemen, — I shall detain you only a few moments more. There are several prominent gentlemen here present from various parts of our beloved country, whose names have been handed to me by the Committee, and whom I shall request to address you upon this occasion. In closing this address I beg to remark that funeral rites are useless to the dead. To the living, however, they are useful. By them we yield to our sense of justice, and willingly pay to the dead that tribute of respect which the jealousies of the human heart cause men, oftentimes, to withhold from the living. At the grave it is that distinguished talents and virtues, viewed apart from the frailties of human life, beam with truthful radiance and demand a holy emulation; and there it is that a voice seems to come from that far away spirit-realm, and, falling upon our ears, admonishes us that "we too are mortal," and bids us to look at the manly form lying in the icy embrace of death; and, seeing the open grave soon to receive the great dead, we let the tender part of nature manifest its supremacy and exert its refining power, as we reach forth the hand of sympathy, and "witness the last scene in the drama of our own earthly life."

Let us this day take courage, sustain the new President, have full faith and a well-grounded hope, and be of good cheer, although we weep at the grave of our martyred Garfield. God in heaven will bless us and our nation, and through these tears and these great sorrows lead us onward to a greater greatness, and to a nobler and an ever-enduring destiny.

And now, King Eternal:

> " We need Thee every hour,
> Most gracious Lord;
> No tender voice like Thine,
> Can peace afford."

And my country

> " Needs Thee every hour;
> Stay Thou near by;
> Temptations lose their power
> When Thou art nigh."

ADDRESS

OF

HONORABLE CHARLES A. PEABODY.

OFFICE ADDRESS:

No. 110 Broadway, New York, N.Y.

Ex-United-States Judge.

ADDRESS.

Judge PEABODY, being called on by the President of the meeting, responded as follows : —

MR. CHAIRMAN, — I thank you for the privilege of speaking on this occasion; for, while in common with many others I might, if left to myself, prefer to indulge the melancholy reflections of the occasion in silence and solitude; yet, as we are to commune socially, and speaking our own sadness is to be the order of the meeting, I would not like to be silent and omit to bear testimony to the respect and affection I felt for our late President while living, or the sorrow I feel that he is dead.

The magnitude of the loss and misfortune to our bereaved country might well make us wish to indulge our feelings in silence. The nation is plunged into the deepest mourning by an event of the most painful character in itself, occurring from a cause which enhances greatly the affliction it brings. The death of our chief magistrate at any time would be grievous, even when occurring in the course of nature, and without circumstances of aggravation, and this would be the case in regard to the person who might for the time be invested with the powers and honors of the office, even when that person had no special claims to our regard otherwise ; but the pangs are greatly increased when the event is the result of crime, and the subject of such a fate possesses the peculiar claims to our esteem and affection which were found in the character of General Garfield.

On such an occasion we are not wont to overlook personal traits of character in contemplating his official eminence and dignity, and forget the man in considering the great chief magistrate. We dwell with melancholy interest on his private virtues, and grieve for him in view of them as if he were dependent on them alone for our interest in him; and when — in addition to the loss of the chief magistrate, eminent and great in that respect and in his private character, in his purposes as well as his achievements — we recall the base means by which he is taken from us, we shrink from the contemplation and are overwhelmed.

Our bereaved country, bleeding at every pore, observes this as a day of mourning and humiliation ; and we do well to note the fact, even at this distance on the ocean, and to unite with countrymen at home and wherever else they may be in appropriate devotions. The life of the deceased, prior to the assault — wonderful in what he had accomplished, in the obstacles he had overcome, and in the absence of all favoring means and circumstances except his own inborn strength of purpose and force of character — so pleasantly summarized and presented to us by you, sir, on consenting to preside at this meeting, would have attracted the attention of all appreciative persons; and this, crowned with an exhibition of the most heroic qualities under trials never surpassed in magnitude, might well have been expected to attract attention beyond the borders of his own broad country.

But the interest the event has occasioned has greatly exceeded what could have been expected in foreign countries, and, as has been said, apparently without exaggeration, has no parallel in the history of the world. The increase in facilities for communication between different and distant countries of the world may be supposed in some measure to account for this, and it does in some measure, no doubt; but it falls greatly short of doing so in full. It was the intrinsic qualities of character exhibited by deceased from early childhood: in orphanage bravely battling with adversity to support himself (almost an infant) and aid his afflicted, widowed mother in a struggle for life in a western wilderness; and rising,

not as by a flight or a fortunate leap, but by care-
fully measured and studied legitimate gradations, to
the position in which he died at the age of fifty
years, the chief governmental magistrate of a nation
of fifty millions of people, than which there is no
higher official position known to man on this earth,—
it was this most remarkable life, crowned by months
of suffering, with heroic fortitude perhaps equally remarkable, that has attracted the interest, sympathy,
and affection of the human family throughout, and
even beyond, the borders of Christian civilization, and
has given to our beloved President a breadth and
strength of admiration seldom enjoyed by man.

It may not be amiss to allude for a moment to
the means by which our affliction has been brought
about; and turning our eyes in that direction we
see that, flagrant and hideous as the act seems, it
lacks some circumstances of aggravation which
might have attended it, and has less enormity than
we might at first glance have supposed. The mis-
erable creature who caused the evil acted alone,
without support from or concert with any one else.
Of this there seems to be no doubt. He alone con-
ceived the purpose and performed the act; and in
it he had no " aid " or " comfort," and no encouragement even, from any other person; so that the guilt
extends to no one else, but rests on him alone. It
might have been worse, therefore, in this respect.

The act, it is plain, has no political significance, and this is a fact of no small importance in estimating the weight of the blow by which we are smitten. I repeat, that the crime is the act of one man, and he obscure and unknown, for any other cause good or bad, and has no color of political significance. I need not say this at home, or even here in addressing Americans; for we know that there are no organizations or bodies of men among us whose energies could be directed to such a purpose; and there is not the slightest belief or pretence that any were concerned in this tragedy. In Europe, whence we are now on our way home, in some countries, combinations and conspiracies against the lives of sovereigns and public men of great eminence do occur; and the fact is so often exhibited to the public mind that the first impression there among persons familiar with those facts might be that this act was the result of concert among malcontents or ill-disposed factions in the country where it occurred. We know well that there was nothing of the kind in the case, and that the worthless Guiteau, now languishing in prison, was the sole author of the idea and of the act, without the aid, support, countenance, sympathy, or (as far as known) approbation of any other human being.

Thus much on the supposition that the actor is in a state of mental sanity which makes him responsible for his conduct. What may be thought of the measure of his guilt is of very little importance; and we might, perhaps, well dispense with all consideration of the subject here. That he was not wholly of sound mind all would seem to agree; and there can be little doubt of the fact. Whether his mental status was sufficient to make him responsible in law for his conduct will be determined by the appropriate tribunal. It is of little importance to us, in this connection, on which side of the line marking the boundary between responsibility and irresponsibility for acts usually criminal his place may be assigned him. One wicked or insane man more or less, in our country, is a matter of little importance to the rest of the fifty millions peopling our shores.

However we may view some of the circumstances attending this sad event, and however in their nature tending to aggravate or diminish the affliction to our beloved country, one source remains to us from which we certainly may derive consolation: I allude to the treatment we have received from other nations, their sovereigns, and citizens occupying the highest political and social positions. From them we have received the kindest possible treatment, and the most marked consideration; and we are at liberty to draw from this fact all the consolation it is intended or calculated to afford. Nothing could surpass in kindness the sympathy and affections expressed for our country, our President, and his sorrowing wife and family; and this, too, by all nations with whom we have connection or intercourse. Nothing could tend more directly to soothe our wounded feelings and mitigate our sorrow than to know that they are appreciated, and that we have the sympathy of those around us in the world whose kindly interest and respect we esteem. From them, and from England especially — to whom more than to any other nation we look, if not as a parent, at least as having a common lineage, mission, and destiny — we have received most gratifying assurances of sympathy and kindness in our affliction. Our debt of affection and gratitude let us be prompt to acknowledge, even in our deepest grief. I am sure we have already in our hearts begun to pay it. May she never be in circumstances to receive payment in kind. In nothing does it touch our hearts so tenderly, perhaps, as in its bestowal on the heart-stricken widow now surviving to be the subject of the prayers and benedictions of all good persons.

ADDRESS

OF

REVEREND H. N. McTYEIRE,

OF NASHVILLE, TENN.,

𝔅𝔦𝔰𝔥𝔬𝔭 𝔬𝔣 𝔱𝔥𝔢 𝔐𝔢𝔱𝔥𝔬𝔡𝔦𝔰𝔱 𝔈𝔭𝔦𝔰𝔠𝔬𝔭𝔞𝔩 ℭ𝔥𝔲𝔯𝔠𝔥 𝔖𝔬𝔲𝔱𝔥.

ADDRESS.

Bishop McTYEIRE, being called for by the Chairman, said : —

MR. CHAIRMAN, — There is sorrow on the sea. It is meet and proper that we be joined in spirit with our fellow-citizens on the land who are to-day burying our late President. I was not of those who elected Mr. Garfield. Born and brought up in the South, and dwelling among mine own people, I felt, with them, a sense of defeat when the choice of the American voters fell on him. And yet I bear testimony to this fact: so many and so great were the personal excellences of the successful candidate, they were readily reconciled to political defeat. The canvass over, and its result ascertained, they said, " This man will not suffer the Republic to be harmed. There is security in his elevation, and breadth and uprightness for all. He will do us good and not evil." And the opening of his career was justifying these hopes, when suddenly and wickedly, and cruelly he was struck down.

Often were congratulations exchanged, that in Mr. Garfield our young men had an example that must be very beneficial; and the crowning of such a life with honor, the highest that the country can bestow, gave wholesome emphasis to that example. Sober, industrious, frugal, upright; not ashamed of poverty, not shunning toil; but rising by self-reliant steps to the foremost place among men. Here is a lesson; here is encouragement; here is a vindication of our social and civil institutions.

And though we have lost him, these are blessings that cannot be lost to the youth of our land. The manner of his life must have an elevating influence upon public men. He was not ashamed of his religious nor of his political principles. True to both, anywhere, everywhere. Even as President of the United States — courted, followed, flattered — we find him, as aforetime, worshipping in one of the humblest conventicles of Washington City; keeping faith with his plain brethren, the Disciples, and with his conscience and his God.

Much prayer has been offered for the wounded President. Our own country, from thousands of hearts and congregations, has sent up daily petitions to heaven. In England and on the Continent, doubtless we were all touched at the feeling shown, and the sympathy for our national calamity. Since the extreme illness of the Prince of Wales, years ago, Great Britain had not been so stirred. Prayers were offered there by sincere souls, and by great assemblies. We left the flags in London and Liverpool, on ships and public buildings, at half mast.

What shall we say now? Shall our great grief be deepened by the taunts of infidelity? Shall it be declared that our God heareth not prayer because the President is dead, for whose spared life so many prayed? Nay, my friends. Verily, our God *is* a prayer-hearing and a prayer-answering God. " Ask, and it shall be given; seek, and ye shall find; knock, and it shall be opened unto you," is still true. God, our Heavenly Father, always reserves and exercises an all-wise, all-loving, and a parental discretion as to the specific manner of granting blessings asked for, and of answering prayers. Were it not so, we, in our ignorance, might well be afraid to ask for any thing. The privilege of petition might turn out a curse if our specific requests were always called down on our heads. When we ask for blessing, a blessing we have, though, may be, not in the precise form that our ignorant and eager desire dictated. Good we seek, and good will be found; but God is to determine the shape and measure of it. These conditions of fervent, effectual prayer remain the same, whether one man, or a thousand, or a nation, is bowed in prayer. Human majorities and multitudes cannot take away this divine discretion, this fatherly prerogative, in answering prayer; and we rejoice that it is so.

All men must die, sooner or later. Prayer cannot make any man live forever, and so escape the doom which He himself hath fixed who appointed prayer. We look to the ends, the uses, the consequences, the circumstances of living or dying, at a particular time, and ask that a valuable life may be spared, in view of these. It may please God to lengthen days; or who can tell if it may not please him to grant the same or greater blessings, in some other way than by lengthening days?

What do we see? The hearts of all Americans united about that sick-bed. On the pulse of the President our fingers have been for these weary, anxious months. Bitterness and strife cease. As was said in the opening prayer, " The hearts of our people have been knit and woven together." God can make the wrath of man to praise him, — out of seeming evil, still educing good. The Sovereign of the British Empire, — whose queenly wisdom and womanly virtue make her to be admired and loved in all lands, and in none more than in our own, — she weeps with the widow of our lamented President, and her people mingle their tears with ours. What a thing is this that has come to pass! President Garfield was in office about six months, and nearly half of that time was spent in tragic sufferings and death. But the longest administration allowed to any President would not have produced such results. The most brilliant decade of government never approached such moral, national, and international achievements. Behold, the ministry of innocent, heroic suffering! God has not allowed it to be in vain. He has heard prayer. Let us sing of mercy and judgment. And let us remember, with bowed hearts and thankful, that while Mr. Garfield was a statesman and patriot, and therefore we had hope in his life, he was also a Christian, and we have hope in his death.

ADDRESS

OF

HONORABLE U. M. ROSE

OF LITTLE ROCK, ARK.,

Judge in the State Courts of Arkansas.

ADDRESS.

Judge Rose, having been called for by the Chairman, said : —

Mr. Chairman, — The subject of our great affliction is the more gloomy to me from the fact that I am not able to see any compensating advantages of any great value to flow from the death of the President. While it may be desirable to take a hopeful view of the situation, it is doubtless still better to take an accurate view. In the infinite number of consequences that must flow directly or indirectly from every important event, it is always possible to make such a selection as will, when separately considered, make it appear that the world has been benefited or injured, just as we please. Naturally shocked by a great crime, the mind seeks relief in some vague theory of collateral advantages. In this case I have not heard of any benefit that can be regarded as of any lasting value. It is creditable to humanity to think that the wounding and death of the President have called forth such universal expressions of sympathy from the whole civilized world; and we who have been abroad during the summer have all, I doubt not, been infinitely touched by the uniform warmth and sincerity of the manifestations of sorrow on the part of people of alien race and speech, as well as by the people of England, in a calamity that seemed to be peculiarly our own; but we all knew before that " one touch of nature makes the whole world kin." A new example can only give some new emphasis to a well-known truism.

The most desirable of all the advantages that I have heard mentioned was, that the death of Mr. Garfield would banish or allay all that sectional strife which — with sad impeachment of our wisdom — has proved so injurious to our country. Figures of speech may certainly be indulged when the heart is full of mourning; but I am glad to apprehend, as a sober reality, that the sectional strife thus to be dispelled has already died a natural death, being now only occasionally galvanized into a semblance of life by the appliances of American politicians. To hope that these politicians will undergo any thorough reformation because of any emotion whatever is to indulge in hopes that are belied by all past experience. It is not unjust to suppose that their sorrow, however sincere, will be tempered or increased by discreet considerations as to how the event may chance to affect their individual interests.

Confronted by a great misfortune, we are brought directly face to face with the question of the existence of evil in the world in a hard and revolting manner. We cannot see how it is that " an eagle, towering in his pride of place," should be " moused at by a hawk, and killed." Darker than any question propounded by the sphinx is this problem that defies our deepest scrutiny. Every one must judge of it as he will; but to me it seems to be almost as irreverent to take Providence under any apparent patronage as to tax eternal justice with blindness or cruelty.

I should be sorry to think that the deep feeling everywhere displayed has been wholly due to the illustrious official position occupied by the deceased. As President of the Republic, Mr. Garfield was entitled to respect; but " a breath can make them, as a breath has made." On a moment's reflection it must be obvious that Garfield will be remembered more as a man than as a President. Having risen from the humblest rank of life to the highest, he was the fit representative of every class of our people. A self-made man, he was of that type that Americans most delight to honor. He was far above the average of our later Presidents ; their equal in statesmanship, their superior in cultivation and scholarship. He had laid his hand to the great work of purifying American politics and of introducing some rational civil service, and the people had faith in his ability to work out the needed reform. Another may carry on the labor with equal intelligence and firmness; but the indefinable and potent spell of individual prestige is gone forever. Is it not true that Sparta hath a thousand better men than he. The death of a good man in high place, competent to perform its duties in a manner suitable to their dignity and importance, is simply irreparable. In spite of all specious pleas, and hopes fondly cherished by us all which may prove delusive, my best conviction is that we are returning home to our country to find it infinitely poorer than it was when we left it.

An ancient philosopher advised that no man should be counted happy until after his death. If President Garfield did not live long enough for his country, he lived long enough for his own fame; and the tragic manner of his death will clothe his life with a deeper and more tender interest. The example of his early struggles and later successes will serve to animate generous spirits yet unborn, while the uncomplaining fortitude of his last long agony, soothed and sustained by all that is bright and beautiful in womanly devotion, will ever remain as a priceless legacy to be cherished by rich and by poor alike.

ADDRESS

OF

HONORABLE EDWARD H. EAST

OF NASHVILLE, TENN.,

𝔈𝔵=𝔍𝔲𝔡𝔤𝔢 𝔦𝔫 𝔱𝔥𝔢 𝔖𝔱𝔞𝔱𝔢 ℭ𝔬𝔲𝔯𝔱𝔰 𝔬𝔣 𝔗𝔢𝔫𝔫𝔢𝔰𝔰𝔢𝔢.

ADDRESS.

Judge EAST, being called for by the Chairman, said : —

MR. CHAIRMAN, — On the 4th of March, 1881, James A. Garfield was inaugurated President of the United States. Among the spectators of this august scene were some who had a peculiar and personal interest in the man and occasion. There was his devoted wife, who had journeyed hand in hand with him from obscurity to the proud elevation he that day reached. There were his hopeful children, and his old mother, who in maternal pride saw her boy advanced by his fellow-citizens to be the first citizen in a republic distinguished for great men. To her this event must have had especial interest, being the consummation of her highest hopes, — an ample recompense for her life of toil and privation. On the 2d of July, 1881, President Garfield was shot down in the streets of Washington.

> " An eagle, towering in his pride of place,
>   Was by a mousing owl hawk'd at, and killed."

65

The sorely-wounded man struggled with his mortal hurt with manful courage and Christian patience for weary days, weeks, and months, and the pathetic combat has been watched with deepest sympathy by the whole civilized world. Emperors, kings, and queens, and more than these, the great masses of humanity, have hung upon the vicissitudes of the sick chamber with keen interest, and alternated with every gleam of hope and fear. All is ended now. The skill of science, the love of friends, the loyalty of people, and the prayers of Christendom have striven in vain to preserve a life so precious.

The civilized world has received the sad news of his death with a shock of sorrow. It is due from us, who were temporary sojourners in foreign lands during these sad days, to bear to our countrymen at home the evidences of the deep and broad sympathy which we have everywhere witnessed in behalf of our deceased President. There was no man or ruler on earth on whom envy or hatred had less cause to fix a malignant and murderous purpose. It seems, in these days, that men of eminence, by whatever official designation they may be called, who attract an unusual share of public affection or notice, are open to the assaults of those who murder from vanity or malice. If we raise up men worthy to represent us, may we not expect that these men should also die for us, rather than die in the usual way? Here was a man who had lately sheathed the sword of a major-general, had for eighteen years been a representative in the Congress of the United States, and before he had laid down this honor he had been crowned with the laurels of a senator, and instantly advanced by his fellow-citizens to the chief magistracy of the nation. Did ever such magnificent prospects lie stretched out in front of any man, in ancient or modern times? And surely the prospect must have been sweetened by the fact that wife, mother, and children were present to participate in and share the joys and honors, as they had in other days borne with him the burdens.

> "This is the state of man: to-day he puts forth
> The tender leaves of hope, to-morrow blossoms,
> And bears his blushing honors thick upon him:
> The third day, comes a frost, a killing frost;
> And — when he thinks, good easy man, full surely
> His greatness is a ripening — nips his root,
> And then he falls."

It is eminently befitting that we — citizens of the Great Republic, whose chief magistrate has thus been "taken off," while the hearts of our country-men are bowed down in sorrow as they deposit the remains of the murdered President in his "narrow home" — should commingle our tears and griefs with theirs, and tender to her who has suffered most the consolations of our sympathies. And, above all, the American citizen should, in view of the open tomb, resolve to free our politics of that party rancor, malice, and hatred which breed and generate the vile instruments of murder and basest crime.

ADDRESS

OF

REV. FATHER M. J. MASTERSON

OF PEABODY, MASS.,

.

Catholic Church in Peabody.

ADDRESS.

MR. CHAIRMAN, *Ladies and Gentlemen, and fellow American Citizens*, — I deem it a duty, to say first of all, that I do not intend, as I am not I hope expected, to stand here before you to address you in any prepared or timely-arranged form of speech. I am here in answer to a well-aimed, I am sure, and gratefully-received invitation, tendered to me but some moments ago, to personally testify that my sorrow and sympathies are cordially united with yours in this sad crisis of our country's trying affliction. I grieve with you for our common loss; our illustrious chief is departed; the great American nation is deeply filled with mourning, and the dear wife and fond children of a faithful husband and father are now plunged into a most hopeless bereavement. And, honored sir, I recall with much pleasure, as a Catholic priest, the living and lively testimony of our church's universal and profound sorrow, as evinced in her early and continued words of cheer to the wounded and dying chief, and in her maternal strains of tenderness for his sufferings and those of his wounded country and family. The Catholic priests and people all over the land prayed as with one mighty voice that the distinguished patient might be spared; that tranquillity might rule our beloved land, and the sting of death be averted from the presidential home. But the tried and brave patriot is gone; the trusted leader of our people has departed; he is torn forever from the free land on whose eminence he had just been seated; taken away from the glory that but yesterday had so completely encircled him; and, worse and worse, dragged from the wife and children he so loved, and that so loved him in return. Let, then, our united sympathy go forth in its most assuaging and hopeful career to cheer our country in her present sadness, and to quench the consuming anguish, as best we can, of poor widowed Mrs. Garfield and her languishing household. Our country's constitution, gentlemen, was once again shocked by the unhallowed hand of the assassin; but it was, thank God, hardly shaken, for it is yet strong and vigorous as before; and so may it ever be a proof against all the future dangers of human frailty with which it may from time to time have to come in conflict.

ADDRESS

OF

GENERAL CYRUS BUSSEY

OF NEW ORLEANS, LA.,

President of the New-Orleans Chamber of Commerce.

ADDRESS.

General BUSSEY, being called upon by the Chairman, said : —

MR. CHAIRMAN, — We have met this day as countrymen of a great nation bowed down under the pressure of a mighty grief; and there can be no doubt that every American regards it a pleasant duty to take part in commemorating this sad event. The Chairman has referred to that which is taking place in our country, and, no doubt, if there is one grief more than another it is that we, as Americans, are this day prohibited from being at home with our countrymen, and sharing with them the great grief that has overspread the nation. I have contemplated for eighty-five days, since the news of that great calamity reached Europe, what must be the feeling as, day by day and hour by hour, the people of our happy, united country have watched the bulletins that have emanated from the sick chamber of our chief magistrate ; and I believe, if it were possible to arrive at an expression of opinion, we would find that the whole American heart is, perhaps for the first time in the history of the nation, beating as one great heart in sympathy over this great calamity which has befallen them. A few months ago it was my good fortune to be in Washington, and in the private chamber of the President's mansion, where I saw a few of the President's friends one by one come in and take him by the hand, — among them *Vice-President* Arthur, who went there to pay his respects to Gen. and Mrs. Garfield, and to congratulate them on their great fortune and prosperity. From that scene, so magnificent, my mind naturally went back to the time when Garfield was a poor boy, one of the lowliest in the land, working at the hardest daily toil to earn support for himself and the widowed mother; and I could not help thinking that it was by Mr. Garfield's own energy and industry, and the practice of those great virtues which characterized the best of our people, he had brought himself from one gradation to another to the proud position of being the head of more than fifty millions of people who did him honor in electing him to that great office. On my way to Europe I again called at the White House, and at that time Mrs. Garfield lay upon a bed of languishing, and was not expected to live. It was the husband's place then to stand at the bedside of his faithful, devoted wife; and he knew how anxiously the American people watched over her sickness, now overshadowed by the present calamity. Mrs. Garfield had barely recovered sufficiently to be able to be removed to Long Branch. Her suffering and dangerous illness was one of the incidents which prepared the public mind for the great sympathy which has been manifested for her since the occurrence of the tragic event. The President had removed his wife to Long Branch, and had returned to Washington for a day or two, and was on his way again to join her when the bullet of the assassin felled him; and for eighty days the prayers of the whole world have gone up as one prayer to Almighty God that he would spare the life of the President, and give him back to the nation and his loving wife, so that he might still be a blessing, and that his life might be an example to the people of the earth. But God willed it otherwise, and there is doubtless a lesson in it all. President Garfield himself believed in an overshadowing Providence; and they well remembered, many of them, — in that dark hour when ABRAHAM LINCOLN was stricken down, and when the people of New York were gathered in the streets, an excited mob, believing that in some way the party opposed to the administration was responsible for the deed, and seeking some person on whom to wreak their vengeance, — it was in such an hour that JAMES A. GARFIELD stepped on to the balcony of a hotel, and called on his countrymen to hear him, and told them that God reigned and would vindicate his law. Again, when Gen. Garfield stood in the burying-ground at Arlington, and made the oration at the dedication of that great sepulchre, he referred to the martyrdom of St. Peter at Rome, and the erection of that magnificent temple, St. Peter's, which had attracted the eyes of two hundred millions of people; he referred to the sacrifice of the humble fisherman who laid down his life; and in that, one of the grandest orations ever delivered in America, he made use of this sentence: — " A noble life, crowned with heroic deeds, rises above and outlives the pride and pomp of glory of the weightiest empire on the earth." Thus recognizing that the life of one man might become of more importance and more value to the world than a whole empire itself. President Garfield's has been such a life. When the historian shall write the life of that great man, and compile his utterances, it will be found that in every public speech there are gems of thought that will do honor to the greatest minds who have ever lived. The whole of his life has been spent in the acquisition of knowledge, and as a teacher of men. He has left on record nothing of which his family and the nation cannot take pride. Education, civilization, and the Christian religion ever found in him a faithful advocate and friend.

I have no doubt that the sickness and death of Gen. Garfield has had more to do in bringing about •a unity of feeling among the nations than any event which has transpired since the crucifixion of Christ. It is impossible to say at present what will be the influence of Gen. Garfield's sickness and death; but we are all well aware that it would have been impossible to have conveyed to the mind of every young man in the nation the lesson of Gen. Garfield's death, but for the crowning event which has made it so glorious. Every young man in the nation, no doubt, has been stimulated by the fact that it is possible for the lowliest man to rise by his own energy to the most exalted station; and what woman in the land has read of the heroic devotion Mrs. Garfield has displayed in the sick chamber without resolving that in future she would become a more devoted wife and mother than she has ever been before? The aspirations of the whole world have no doubt been elevated. What grander compliment could be paid to a great statesman, in a country like America, than is contained in the announcement which has been made that, after twenty-five years of public life, surrounded as he has been by corruption, with the opportunity of amassing a large fortune without the knowledge of any one, the amount he has left behind him is so small? The people of the United States have exhausted the entire market of every thing that will exhibit their feeling of grief, and entire streets of the great cities are draped in mourning; not a house being without some evidence of the sorrow that is felt by the people. The great marts of trade are closed; around every hearthstone, and in every temple of worship in America and in foreign lands, the people are bowed to-day in sorrow. Witness the part taken in this great sorrow by the people of England, from the Queen to the humblest peasant; and we are sure there is not a man among them coming from the other side of the Atlantic who, after all the evidences received from the voice of England, did not feel he had come back to the old homestead to share the sympathies of the English people in this great calamity. The people of Great Britain, I wish to say as an American, have stamped themselves as the greatest people on the civilized globe. They have carried into every land, by their magnificent commerce, civilization and Christianity, which has blessed the world to a greater degree than the influence of any other nation on the earth. It is no small matter to receive the sympathy of such a people. The Mayor of Liverpool said the other day, at the Town-hall, in his eloquent speech, that they were there to sympathize with their kinsmen. They were kinsmen. That Americans were English, and he had no doubt that England was American, and that from that time forward a new era had dawned between the two nations, and that whatever in the past had tended to divide and distract them, they were from this time forward one great Anglo-Saxon people, — one in sentiment and one in mind. In conclusion, MR. PRESIDENT, I beg to present for consideration and action, upon this sad and solemn occasion, the following resolutions : —

Resolved, That all American citizens now on board the steam-ship "SCYTHIA" share with their countrymen and with the world the horror and detestation of the crime which has stricken down the President of the United States ; that we cannot adequately express the anguish we feel at the death of so distinguished a man at the beginning of a term of service which promised to bring into play his noblest qualities, and to mark a new epoch in the administration of the government ; that we look with melancholy pride as well upon the rare fortitude and Christian patience with which he endured extreme and prolonged pain as upon the lofty attributes of his character as statesman and as man ; and that we tender our profound sympathy with Mrs. Garfield, who from first to last has shown the best attributes of womanhood, and with the other members of a family who have thus cruelly been robbed of their head.   And be it further

Resolved, That we desire to express our grateful appreciation of the sorrow and sympathy evinced by all classes in Great Britain, from Queen to peasant, with the late President in his suffering, with his family in their bereavement, and with the Republic in its grief ; that we especially recognize the depth and sincerity of the feeling manifested by the people of Europe at every stage of the agony which culminated in death, and on the occasion of the loss which death entails ; that we value highly these evidences of affection and respect, and that we discern in the spontaneity and warmth of their display, and in the response they call forth from the American heart, the development of a force that will hereafter be beneficially felt in the relations of the two countries, England and America.

Before taking my seat, Mr. Chairman, permit me to say that, while we pause before the open grave of our dead President, where very soon his remains are to be forever hid from our view, and because of the wise provision made by our fathers in the establishment of our government, another has taken upon himself the great office of President, and has issued a proclamation and an inaugural address which are filled with the highest evidences of his ability and fitness for the exalted office he holds. *President* ARTHUR has had large experience, and has shown great executive ability; and has shown that he possesses a conscience ever ready to respect the will of his countrymen. I was pained to read in the public journals of England apprehensions that a corrupt party was coming into power in the American Republic. These journals know very little of our institutions if they suppose the American people will tolerate a corrupt government. The struggle for office is everywhere fierce and exciting; but when the contest is over, the incumbent is answerable to the people, who will see that the government is faithfully administered. In this trying hour *President* ARTHUR deserves the sympathy and support of the whole American people, whose love of country should rise above personal considerations. And, MR. PRESIDENT, I now ask you to submit the resolutions which have been read to this large gathering of Americans and of Europeans for their adoption and approval, after they have been, as I trust they will be, seconded by some gentleman present in an appropriate address.

THE RESOLUTIONS, as offered by *General* BUSSEY, were seconded by Hon. F. A. WARD, of the city of Brooklyn, N.Y., in an effective and eloquent address, which was listened to with marked attention; after which they were submitted by the Chairman to the assembly, and were *unanimously* adopted, in the midst of sad hearts and eyes filled with tears of grief.

THE addresses having been made and the resolutions adopted, the following NATIONAL HYMN, having been announced by Rev. JOHN P. NEWMAN, D.D., was sung, producing profound impressions : —

"MY COUNTRY! 'TIS OF THEE."

My country! 'tis of thee,
Sweet land of liberty,
  Of thee I sing:
Land where my fathers died,
Land of the pilgrims' pride,
From every mountain's side
  Let freedom ring.

My native country! thee —
Land of the noble free —
  Thy name I love:
I love thy rocks and rills,
Thy woods and templed hills;
My heart with rapture thrills,
  Like that above.

Let music swell the breeze,
And ring from all the trees
  Sweet freedom's song:
Let mortal tongues awake,
Let all that breathe partake,
Let rocks their silence break,
  The sound prolong.

Our fathers' God, to thee —
Author of liberty —
  To thee we sing:
Long may our land be bright
With freedom's holy light.
Protect us by thy might,
  Great God, our King!

THE Hon. AUGUSTUS BELMONT, of New York City, delivered an ADDRESS in the order stated on page 7 hereof, which was of rare classical beauty and touchingly appropriate to the occasion, and it was attentively listened to by the large audience ; but a written copy of it has not been furnished for publication with the foregoing proceedings, which is much regretted by the SECRETARY, as no doubt it will be by those into whose hands this MEMORIAL may come.

THE SECRETARY also regrets that the Hon. F. A. WARD did not furnish a written copy of his excellent and appropriate address for publication herein.

AT the request of a very large number of passengers on board the " SCYTHIA," these memorial proceedings have been published in the present form, together with " *list of* SALOON PASSENGERS."

LEWIS C. LILLIE,
Secretary,
Nos. 6 and 7 Bowdoin Square,
Boston, Mass.

LIST OF SALOON PASSENGERS.

LIST OF SALOON PASSENGERS, PER ROYAL MAIL STEAMSHIP "SCYTHIA,"

(CAPT. MURPHY,)

LIVERPOOL TO NEW YORK, SEPT. 24, 1881.

Mr. A. Ajuria.

Miss Louisa Bain.

Mr. Leon Backer.

Mr. A. C. Baldwin, Boston, Mass.

Mr. George Barclay, New York, N.Y.

Mr. H. J. Barrett.

Mr. E. L. Baylies.

Mrs. N. E. Baylies, New York, N.Y.

Miss Baylies.

Miss N. Baylies.

Mr. James J. Belden, Syracuse, N.Y.

Mrs. Jas. J. Belden, Syracuse, N.Y.

Hon. AUGUSTUS BELMONT and man-servant, New York, N.Y.

Miss Benogh.

Mr. George C. Boden, Atlantic City, N.J.

Mr. S. Boileau, Easton, Penn.

Mrs. Boileau, Easton, Penn.

Mrs. BOLTON, child, and maid.

Mr. Christian Börs, New York, N.Y.

Mrs. Christian Börs, New York, N.Y.

Mr. B. Börs, New York, N.Y.

Rev. R. Russell Booth, D.D., New York, N.Y.

Mrs. R. Russell Booth, New York, N.Y.

Mr. A. Boyle.

Rev. F. W. Braithwaite, Stamford, Conn.

Miss Brandies.

Mr. M. Bray, Boston, Mass.

F. Brunning, M.D., Cincinnati, O.

Gen. CYRUS BUSSEY, New Orleans, La.

Miss Butterworth, New York, N.Y.

Mr. Franci C. Cantine, New York, N.Y.

Mr. J. W. Clark.

Mr. George Clark.

Mr. W. C. Clark.

Mrs. H. C. Clarkener, St. Louis, Mo.

Miss Clarkener, St. Louis, Mo.

Mr. J. D. Clarkener, St. Louis, Mo.

Mr. James Coats.

Mrs. Coats.

Miss Coats.

Miss A. Coats.

Miss Alice Coats.

Mr. S. Coats.

Mr. J. Coats, jun.

Mr. F. Coats, man-servant, and maid-servant.

Miss Flora E. Cole, Baltimore, Md.

Mr. A. E. Connover, New York, N.Y.

Mrs. A. E. Connover, New York.

Mr. W. H. Cook.

Miss H. Courtis.

Dr. Craig.

Mrs. Craig.

Mr. O. Cranz.

Miss Cropp.

Mr. James C. Davis, Boston, Mass.

Mrs. James C. Davis, Boston, Mass.

Miss Nellie Davis, Boston, Mass.

Mr. John H. Davis and man-servant, New York, N.Y.

Mrs. John H. Davis, New York, N.Y.

Mr. Horace Demming, New York, N.Y.

Mr. R. B. Dobie.

Mr. E. J. Dougherty.

Mrs. Dougherty.

Mr. E. Duvivier.

Hon. EDWARD H. EAST, Nashville, Tenn.

Mrs. EDWARD H. EAST, Nashville, Tenn.

Mr. C. R. Eaton.

Mrs. Eaton.

Rev. Dr. Eccleston.

Mr. J. Clinton Edgar, New York, N.Y.

Mrs. George W. Elder and maid.

Miss L. W. Elder.

Mr. J. A. Fairfax, San Francisco, Cal.

Mrs. C. J. Fairfax, San Francisco, Cal.

Miss A. S. E. Fairfax, San Francisco, Cal.

Miss A. C. Fairfax, San Francisco, Cal.

Mrs. Fentress.

Miss Fentress.

Miss Fentress.

Mrs. M. R. Field.

A. Fleming, M.D., Pittsburg, Penn.

Mrs. A. Fleming, Pittsburg, Penn.

Mr. W. R. Fortune.

Mr. Francis B. Foster, New York, N.Y.

Mr. Edward J. Fox, Easton, Penn.

Mrs. Edward J. Fox, Easton, Penn.

Miss Fox, Easton, Penn.

Rev. John Fox.

Mr. J. F. Freeman.

Mr. A. Gailliard.

Miss Mary Glover.

Mrs. A. Goldsmith, New York, N.Y.

Mr. Goldsmith.

Mr. Harry B. Grey, Brooklyn, N.Y.

Miss J. B. Greene, Buffalo, N.Y.

Mr. Thomas Greenlees.

Mr. H. W. Hammond, Liverpool, Eng.

Mr. Sampson Hanbury, Meldon, Eng.

Mr. Alfred Hardie, Manitoba, Can.

Miss Hardie.

Mrs. S. Henry and child.

Miss F. Henry.

Mr. C. Henry.

Hr. W. H. Herriman.

Mrs. W. H. Herriman.

Mr. W. Hidden.

Mr. Edward Hill.

Mr. Fred. Hill.

Miss Hill.

Miss Hinshelwood.

Mr. C. J. Hirst.

Mr. N. B. Hogg, jun., Pittsburg, Penn.

Mr. F. L. Holmquist, New York, N.Y.

Mrs. F. L. Holmquist, two children, and maid, New York, N.Y.

Mr. F. J. Hotop.

Miss Meta Huger.

Miss Huguenin.

Mr. L. Hurbutt.

Miss L. Hussey.

Mr. J. S. Huyler.

Miss James.

Mr. S. J. Jervey.

Mr. Henry W. Johnson, New York, N.Y.

Mrs. Henry W. Johnson, New York, N.Y.

Mr. D. H. Joostin, New York, N.Y.

Mr. A. D. Julliard, New York, N.Y.

Mrs. A. D. Julliard, New York, N.Y.

Mr. Horace Kelley, Cleveland, O.

Mrs. Horace Kelley, Cleveland, O.

Rev. JAMES M. KING, D.D., New York, N.Y.

Mrs. JAMES M. KING, New York, N.Y.

Mrs. M. H. Kinney.

Miss Kinney.

Miss Lathrop.

Mrs. E. W. Landon, three children, and governess, New York, N.Y.

Mr. D. G. Leggett.

Miss H. Legorju.

Mr. LEWIS C. LILLIE, New York and Boston.

Mr. W. H. Lippincott.

Mr. E. H. Lockyer, Bristol, Eng.

Rev. M. J. MASTERSON, Peabody, Mass.

Miss H. Mather.

Mr. John McKee, New York, N.Y.

Rev. M. T. McManus.

Rev. H. N. McTyeire, Nashville, Tenn.

Miss McTyeire, Nashville, Tenn.

Mr. Alanlo Miams, Bristol, Eng.

Mr. T. B. Mills.

Mrs. T. B. Mills, three children, and servant.

Mr. A. Minis, jun., New York, N.Y.

Mr. W. J. Mitchell.

Mr. Peter Moller, jun.

Mrs. Peter Moller.

Miss Moller.

Mr. E. C. Moller.

Miss Sarah Morrow, New York, N.Y.

Miss Eliza Mote.

Alexander Muirhead, M.D., London, Eng.

Mr. Henry James Muirhead, London, Eng.

Miss L. M. Nathurst.

Mr. William James Neill, New York, N.Y.

Mrs. William James Neill, New York, N.Y.

Rev. John P. Newman, D.D., New York, N.Y.

Mrs. John P. Newman, New York, N.Y.

Hon. Marcus P. Norton and man-servant, New York and Boston.

Miss Carrie T. Newman, New York, N.Y.

Mrs. T. B. Oakley.

Miss N. O'Donohue.

Sister M. J. O'Donohue.

Sister M. S. O'Malley.

Mr. J. B. Palmer, Concord, N.H.

Mrs. J. B. Palmer, Concord, N.H.

Mrs. G. H. Palmer, Concord, N.H.

Miss A. Parker.

Mr. M. Paton.

Hon Charles A. Peabody, New York, N.Y.

Mrs. Charles A. Peabody, New York, N.Y.

Professor J. M. Peirce.

Mr. C. Pennington.

Mr. C. C. Perkins.

Mr. C. B. Perkins.

Mr. J. Lamb Perry.

Miss L. Phillips, New York, N.Y.

Dr. H. Pickney.

Mrs. H. C. Plass, New York, N.Y.

Mr. T. T. Randolph.

Miss L. Randolph.

Miss E. Randolph.

Miss L. T. Randolph.

Mr. J. H. Richmond.

Mr. C. B. Robinson, London, Eng.

John A. Rogers, M.D., Paterson, N.J.

Mr. John G. Rollins, London, Eng.

Mrs. John G. Rollins, London, Eng.

Miss Rollins, London, Eng.

Miss Rollins, London, Eng.

Hon. U. M. Rose, Little Rock, Ark.

Mr. J. Rosenthal, New York, N.Y.

Mrs. J. Rosenthal, New York, N.Y.

Miss Rosenthal, New York, N.Y.

Mr. John L. Ross, Cambridge, Mass.

Mrs. John L. Ross, Cambridge, Mass.

Mr. Denham Ross.

Miss Rubino and maid.

Mr. Rubino.

Mr. Stillwell H. Russell, Austin, Tex.

Miss Ryder.

Mr. L. Sabriskie.

Mr. N. E. Sainsbury.

Madame Santin.

Rev. Horace D. Sassaman, Erwinna, Penn.

Miss Sawyer.

Mr. William J. Sawyer, Allegheny City, Penn.

Mrs. John Scott, child, and maid.

Mr. E. Shannon, Norfolk, Va.

Mr. S. J. Sheil.

Miss N. Shoemaker.

Miss M. E. Shoemaker.

Miss B. Shoemaker.

Mr. A. Shrewsbury.

Mr. E. Siegel.

Mr. J. Sillem, Amsterdam, Holland.

Mr. I. W. Spiegelberg.

Miss H. Stern, St. Louis, Mo.

Miss Fannie Stern, St. Louis, Mo.

Mr. Byam K. Stevens, New York, N.Y.

Mrs. Byam K. Stevens, New York, N.Y.

Mr. K. Stevens, New York, N.Y.

Mr. Hugh A. Stirling.

Mr. J. H. Strahan.

Mrs. J. H. Strahan.

Miss Strahan.

Mr. T. W. Strong.

Miss M. Stump.

Mr. R. B. Symington, New York, N.Y.

Mrs. R. B. Symington, child, and maid.

Mr. Richard Synnot, Melbourne, Victoria, Australia.

Mr. Daniel Talmage, New York, N.Y.

Rev. D. A. Tivenan, Brooklyn, N.Y.

Dr. H. Tuholske.

Mrs. H. Tuholske, child, and maid.

Mr. Edmund Tweedale.

Mr. C. T. H. Vagt.

Mr. L. Vasquez.

Mr. E. Vedder.

Mrs. E. Vedder and two children.

Mr. J. W. Vernon.

Professor J. M. Van Vleck.

Hon. F. A. Ward, Brooklyn, N.Y.

Mrs. F. A. Ward, Brooklyn, N.Y.

Miss M. Ward, Brooklyn, N.Y.

Lieut.-Col. Wickham.

Mr. Alan Williams.	Mrs. Woodside.
Mr. C. W. Winfield, Beaver Dam, Wis.	Miss Woodside.
Mrs. C. W. Winfield, Beaver Dam, Wis.	Mr. B. W. Woodward, Lawrence, Kansas.
Mr. T. Wolfe, jun., New Orleans, La.	Mrs. B. W. Woodward.
	Mrs. Wyckoff.
Mrs. Womersly.	Miss H. Yorke.
	Miss M. Yorke.

www.ingramcontent.com/pod-product-compliance
Lightning Source LLC
Chambersburg PA
CBHW020032030726
47499CB00007B/2385